How to Make a Pancake

TREASURE BAY

Parent's Introduction

Welcome to **We Read Phonics**! This series is designed to help you assist your child in reading. Each book includes a story, as well as some simple word games to play with your child. The games focus on the phonics skills and sight words your child will use in reading the story.

Here are some recommendations for using this book with your child:

1 Word Play

There are word games both before and after the story. Make these games fun and playful. If your child becomes bored or frustrated, play a different game or take a break.

Phonics is a method of sounding out words by blending together letter sounds. However, not all words can be "sounded out." **Sight words** are frequently used words that usually cannot be sounded out.

2 Read the Story

After some word play, read the story aloud to your child—or read the story together, by reading aloud at the same time or by taking turns. As you and your child read, move your finger under the words.

Next, have your child read the entire story to you while you follow along with your finger under the words. If there is some difficulty with a word, either help your child to sound it out or wait about five seconds and then say the word.

3 Discuss and Read Again

After reading the story, talk about it with your child. Ask questions like, "What happened in the story?" and "What was the best part?" It will be helpful for your child to read this story to you several times. Another great way for your child to practice is by reading the book to a younger sibling, a pet, or even a stuffed animal!

This time, let's read the story together!

LEVEL 3

Level 3 introduces words with long "a" and long "i" (as in *late* and *like*), as well as the vowel combinations "er," "ir," and "ur" (as in *her, sir,* and *fur*). Other letter combinations include "qu" (as in *quick*), "sh" (as in *shine*), "th" (as in *math*), "ch" (as in *church*), and "tch" (as in *match*).

How to Make a Pancake

A We Read Phonics™ Book
Level 3

_____

Text Copyright © 2010 by Treasure Bay, Inc.
Illustrations Copyright © 2010 by Jeffrey Ebbeler

Reading Consultants: Bruce Johnson, M.Ed., and Dorothy Taguchi, Ph.D.

We Read Phonics™ is a trademark of Treasure Bay, Inc.

Published by
Treasure Bay, Inc.
P.O. Box 119
Novato, CA 94948 USA

Printed in Singapore

Library of Congress Catalog Card Number: 2009929513

Hardcover ISBN: 978-1-60115-317-3
Paperback ISBN: 978-1-60115-318-0
PDF E-Book ISBN: 978-1-60115-582-5

We Read Phonics™
Patent Pending

Visit us online at:
www.TreasureBayBooks.com

PR-1-12

How to Make a Pancake

By Dave Max

Illustrated by Jeffrey Ebbeler

Making Words

Creating words using certain letters will help your child read this story.

Materials:

Option 1—Fast and Easy: To print the game materials from your computer, go online to www.WeReadPhonics.com, then go to this book title and click on the link to "View & Print: Game Materials."

Option 2—Make Your Own: You'll need thick paper or cardboard, crayon or marker, and scissors. Cut 2 x 2 inch squares from the paper or cardboard and print these letters and letter combinations on the squares: a, i, e, er, sh, ch, tt, b, c, k, l, m, n, p, s, t.

1. Place the cards letter side up in front of your child. Ask your child to make and say words using the letters available. For example, your child could choose the letters "c," "a," "k," and "e," and make the word *cake*.

2. If needed, you can present certain letters, for example "l," "a," "t," and "e," and ask your child to make *late*. You can also ask your child to add a letter and make *plate*.

3. Try to make as many words that end with "-an," "-ip," "-ake," ate," "-ice," "-er," and "-ike" as possible. Some of these patterns are used in this story. Possible answers include *man, pan, lip, bake, make, mice, nice, litter, batter,* and *like*.

Sight Word Game

Memory

First!

OK, now pick another card.

This is a fun way to practice recognizing some sight words used in the story.

Materials:

Option 1—Fast and Easy: To print the game materials from your computer, go online to www.WeReadPhonics.com, then go to this book title and click on the link to "View & Print: Game Materials."

Option 2—Make Your Own: You'll need 18 index cards and a marker. Write each word listed on the right on two cards. You will now have two sets of cards.

1 Using one set of cards, ask your child to repeat each word after you. Shuffle both decks of cards together, and arrange the cards face down in a grid pattern.

2 The first player turns over one card and says the word, then turns over a second card and says the word. If the cards match, the player takes those cards and continues to play. If they don't match, both cards are turned over, and it's the next player's turn.

3 Keep the cards. You can make more cards with other **We Read Phonics** books and combine the cards for even bigger games!

would

you

or

first

now

into

have

put

mice

3

Would you like to
make a pancake?

If so, get Mom or
Dad to help you.

Or get mice to help!

First get an egg.

Then get a cup
of pancake mix.

Crack the egg in
a dish. Mix well.

Now add the pancake mix.

Mix it into the egg well.

Now add a cup of milk.

Mix in the milk.

You now have pancake batter!

Now get a pan.

Melt butter in the pan.

Put in a bit of batter.

Check to see if the top is wet.

When it is not wet, flip it!

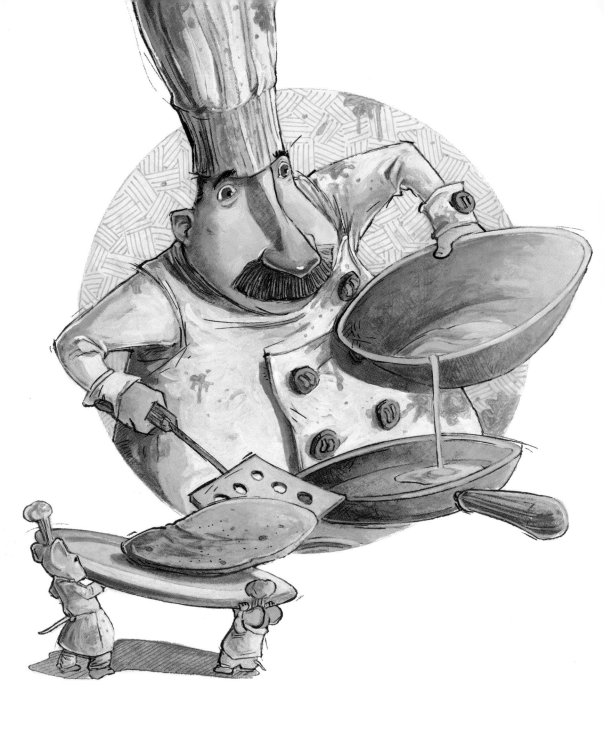

Put the pancake on a plate.

Make a big stack.

Put a pat of butter on top.

Cut up a plum to put on top.

Tuck in a big napkin.

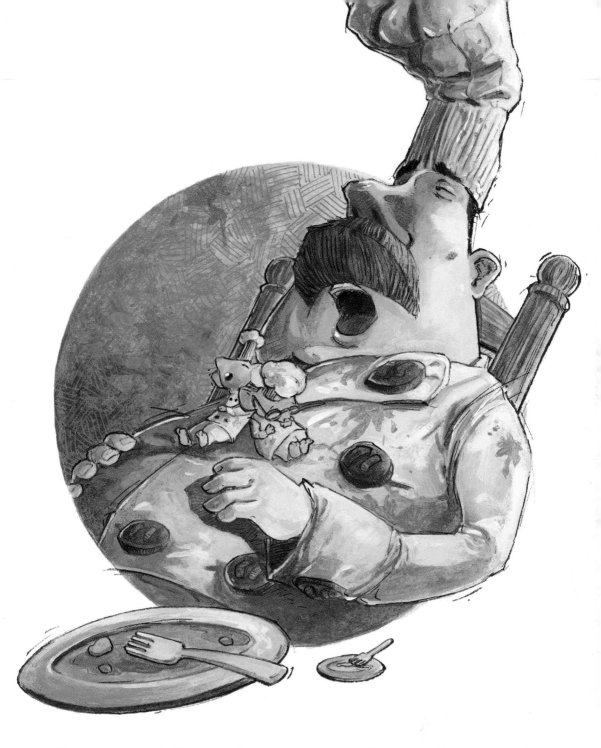

If you like, have a big bunch.

Phonics Game

Taking a Trip

Recognizing final sounds helps readers learn to read new words.

Can you think of a word that ends with the sound nnnn?

Run!

1. Explain to your child that the words *pan, man,* and *napkin* all end with the sound "n." (Instead of saying the letter, make the sound for "n.")

2. Say: "I am taking a trip. You can join me if you can think of a word that ends with the sound 'n.' (Make the sound for 'n.') Can you think of a word that ends with the sound 'n'?" Correct answers can include words from the book or words outside of the book that end with the "n" sound.

3. If your child has trouble, offer some possible answers or repeat step 1.

4. When your child is successful, repeat step 2 with these final letter sounds: d, g, k, l, m, p, t, x, and z.

Phonics Game

First I Heard

First I heard the sound mmmm . . .

Mix in the milk

This is a fun way to practice breaking words into parts, which helps children learn to read new words.

1 Choose a simple three-letter word from the story.

2 Say: "Here is the word . . . (say the word). First, I heard this sound (say the sound for the first letter). Then, I heard this sound (say the sound). Then, I heard this sound (say the sound). For example, for the word *mom,* say: "Here is the word *mom.* First, I heard "m" (say the sound for the letter "m"), then I heard "o" (say the sound of the short "o") then I heard "m" (say the sound for "m").

3 Choose another simple three-letter word from the story. Say the word. Then, ask your child to say the three separate sounds in the word.

4 Continue with additional simple three- or four-letter words from the story. Possible words include *like, make, get, dad, mice, help, mix,* and *dish.*

If you liked *How to Make a Pancake,*
here is another **We Read Phonics** book you are sure to enjoy!

Ant in Her Pants

What if an ant got in your pants? Would it drive you crazy? An odd little ant causes lots of craziness in this very funny book that will leave beginning readers smiling.